# One of Our Tigers is Missing!

by Sue Graves and Pauline Reeves

**W**

## FRANKLIN WATTS
LONDON•SYDNEY

Ted and Ava loved tigers. They had lots of books about tigers and they loved to read about them and talk about them.

"You'll be experts if you keep reading," said Dad.

Ted and Ava were pleased.

They wanted to be tiger experts.

On their birthday, Gran gave them tickets
to the safari park.

"You can go and see the tigers," she said.

"Cool," said Ava. "Tigers are the best."

The next day, they went to the safari park.

"What shall we go and see first?" asked Dad.

"Tigers!" shouted Ava and Ted.

"The tiger enclosure is near here," said Mum, looking at the map. "Let's go there now. We can see the other animals later."

The tigers were in a big enclosure.

It had a wire fence all around it.

"The animals have plenty of room
to run around," said Mum.

"Tigers need a lot of space," said Ava.

"They run very fast."

"If we wait quietly we might see some,"
said Dad.

TIGERS
DO NOT
ENTER!

7

Just then, they saw a park ranger.

He looked worried.

He was talking on his walkie-talkie.

"I can't see her," he said. "I can't see her at all.

Where do you think she can be?"

"What's the matter?" asked Ted.

"We're looking for a female tiger,"
said the park ranger. "She's been missing
for two days. We're worried that she may be
hurt. There might be some sharp wire
on the far side of the field. She may have cut
her leg."

"Don't worry," said Ava. "A tiger's lick
can heal cuts."

"You know a lot about tigers," said the ranger.

"We're experts," said Ava. "Can we help you
look for her?"

"I could do with some help," said the ranger.

"My name is Andy. Come on. Get in the jeep."

Everyone got into Andy's jeep.

"The tiger might have escaped," said Ted.

"Have you looked for footprints

in the rest of the park?"

"Yes," said Andy. 'We don't think

she's escaped. Have you got any other ideas?"

"Tigers need to drink a lot," said Ava.

"Have you looked by the pond?"

"No," said Andy. "That's a good idea.

Let's look there."

13

Andy drove the jeep to the far side of the field.

They could see the pond on the other side

of the fence.

"Look in the bushes," said Ava.

"She might be hiding there."

There was no sign of the missing tiger.

"Oh dear," said Andy, sadly. "She's not there.

Where can she be?"

Suddenly, Ava had an idea.

"Female tigers hide in the shade
when they have cubs," she said.

"Yes," said Ted, excitedly. "Good idea, Ava.
Perhaps the tiger has had cubs.
We should look near the trees."

"Tigers are stripy so they can hide easily," said Ava. "They can be hard to spot."
"You're right," said Andy. "Let's look in the woods."

The woods were dark and shady.

Everyone looked carefully for signs of the tiger.

Just then, Ava spotted something moving.

"Look there!" she cried, pointing to

some long grass. "I think it's a tiger."

18

"It *is* a tiger!" said Andy. "And look, she has

three cubs with her. Thanks for your help.

When you grow up, you'll be good rangers."

"That's just what we want to be," said Ted.

"We want to look after tigers."

"Tigers are the best," said Ava, happily.

# Story order

Look at these 5 pictures and captions.
Put the pictures in the right order
to retell the story.

**1**

The tiger was not by the pond.

**2**

The family went to the safari park.

**3**

The tiger had three cubs.

**4**

The park ranger looked worried.

**5**

Ted and Ava wanted to help the ranger.

# Independent Reading

This series is designed to provide an opportunity for your child to read on their own. These notes are written for you to help your child choose a book and to read it independently.

In school, your child's teacher will often be using reading books which have been banded to support the process of learning to read. Use the book band colour your child is reading in school to help you make a good choice. *One of Our Tigers is Missing!* is a good choice for children reading at Gold Band in their classroom to read independently.

The aim of independent reading is to read this book with ease, so that your child enjoys the story and relates it to their own experiences.

## About the book

Ted and Ava love tigers. When Gran buys them tickets to the safari park, they are very excited to see the tigers. And when they find that one of the tigers has been missing for two days, their expert knowledge helps Andy the ranger to solve the mystery of her whereabouts.

## Before reading

Help your child to learn how to make good choices by asking:
"Why did you choose this book? Why do you think you will enjoy it?"
Look at the cover together and ask: "What do you think the story will be about?" Ask your child to think of what they already know about the story context. Then ask your child to read the title aloud. Ask: "Where do you think this story is taking place?" Remind your child that they can sound out the letters to make a word if they get stuck.

Decide together whether your child will read the story independently or read it aloud to you.

## During reading

Remind your child of what they know and what they can do independently. If reading aloud, support your child if they hesitate or ask for help by telling the word. If reading to themselves, remind your child that they can come and ask for your help if stuck.

## After reading

Support comprehension by asking your child to tell you about the story. Use the story order puzzle to encourage your child to retell the story in the right sequence, in their own words. The correct sequence can be found on the next page.

Help your child think about the messages in the book that go beyond the story and ask: "How are Ted and Ava able to help the ranger? How have they become such experts on tigers?"

Give your child a chance to respond to the story: "What really interests you? What would you like to do when you're an adult?"

## Extending learning

Help your child predict other possible scenarios for the story by asking: "What would happen if a different animal had gone missing? Would the children look for the same clues to trace the missing animal? What clues would be the same for all animals?"

In the classroom, your child's teacher may be teaching contractions. There are many examples in this book that you could look at together, including *let's* (let us), *can't* (cannot), *what's* (what is), *we're* (we are), *don't* (do not), *she's* (she is), *you're* (you are), *it's* (it is), *that's* (that is). Find these together and point out how the apostrophes are used in place of the omitted letters.

Franklin Watts
First published in Great Britain in 2018
by The Watts Publishing Group

Copyright © The Watts Publishing Group 2018
All rights reserved.

Series Editors: Jackie Hamley and Melanie Palmer
Series Advisors: Dr Sue Bodman and Glen Franklin
Series Designer: Peter Scoulding

A CIP catalogue record for this book is
available from the British Library.

ISBN 978 1 4451 6247 8 (hbk)
ISBN 978 1 4451 6249 2 (pbk)
ISBN 978 1 4451 6248 5 (library ebook)

Printed in China

Franklin Watts
An imprint of
Hachette Children's Group
Part of The Watts Publishing Group
Carmelite House
50 Victoria Embankment
London EC4Y 0DZ

An Hachette UK Company
www.hachette.co.uk

www.franklinwatts.co.uk

FSC
www.fsc.org
MIX
Paper from
responsible sources
FSC® C104740

**Answer to Story order: 2, 4, 5, 1, 3**